For Peter and
Laura
—A.S.C.

HarperCollins®, ♣®, and I Can Read Book® are trademarks of HarperCollins Publishers.

Library of Congress Cataloging-in-Publication Data is available.
ISBN-10: 0-06-074170-8 (trade bdg.) — ISBN-13: 978-0-06-074170-9 (trade bdg.)
ISBN-10: 0-06-074171-6 (lib. bdg.) — ISBN-13: 978-0-06-074171-6 (lib. bdg.)
Typography by John Sazaklis
1 2 3 4 5 6 7 8 9 10 ❖ First Edition

Biscuit and the Little Pup

story by ALYSSA SATIN CAPUCILLI
pictures by PAT SCHORIES

HarperCollins*Publishers*

Here, Biscuit.

It's time to play.

Woof, woof!

You found your ball, Biscuit.

Arf!

You found a little pup, too.

Woof, woof!

Come out, little pup.

What is your name?

Woof, woof!

Come out, little pup.

Biscuit wants to play!

Woof, woof!

Arf!

The little pup does not want
to come out.

Here, little pup.

Biscuit has a ball.

Woof, woof!

Biscuit has a bone.

Woof, woof!

Won't you come out,

little pup?

Arf! Arf!

The little pup does not want
to come out yet.

What will we do now?

Woof!

Wait, Biscuit.

Where are you going?

Woof, woof!

Silly puppy!

It's not time for you to hide.

Arf! Arf! Arf! Arf!

Woof, woof!

Oh, Biscuit!

Here comes the little pup!

Woof, woof!

Arf! Arf!

Funny puppies!

You both want to play.

You want to play
hide-and-seek!

Woof, woof!

Ready or not, sweet puppies,

we found both of you!

Arf! Arf!

Woof!